JUNETEENTH

Written by **Van G. Garrett** • Illustrated by **Reginald C. Adams** and **Samson Bimbo Adenugba**

VERSIFY
An Imprint of HarperCollins Publishers

We loaded the car
in search of sounds and stars.

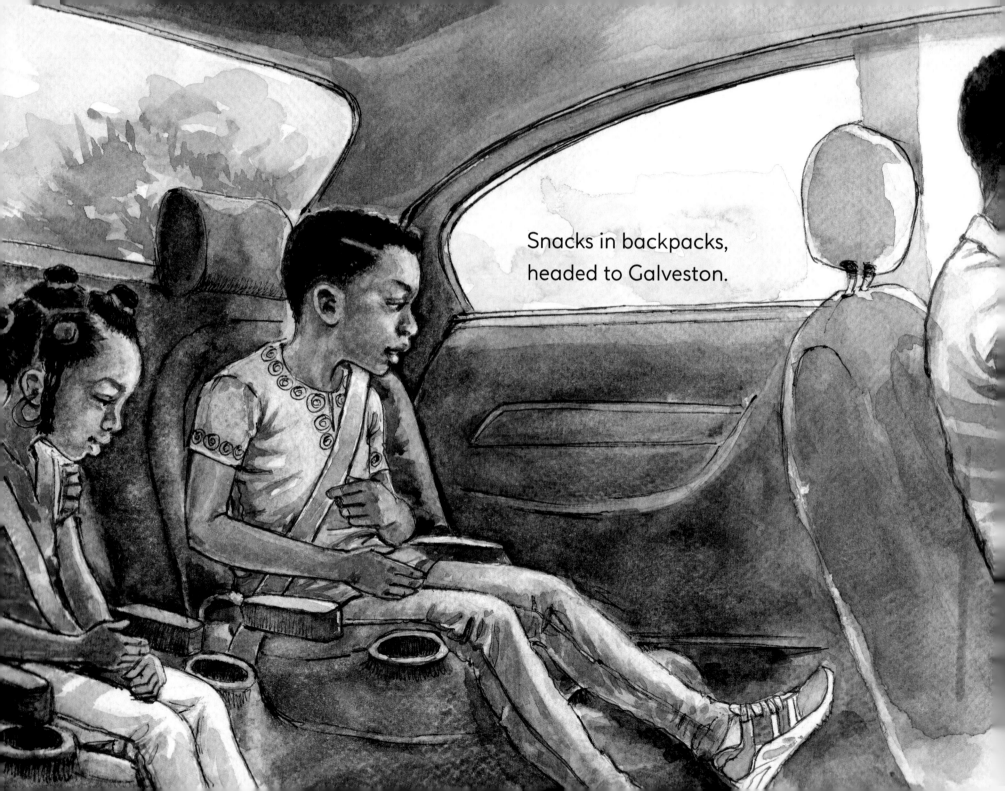

Snacks in backpacks,
headed to Galveston.

Looking for the perfect spot,
we parked and walked,
laughed and talked,
until we got to the *The Strand*.

People smiled and waved
as my wagon bumped
down the street.

My cool shades, shiny mirrors,
blocked the bright Texas sun.

I think this is a good spot,
Dad said, smiling at Mom.

What do you think, Son?

I nodded as Mom reached in a bag
and removed a wrapped sandwich.

I was about to eat
when music filled the street.

Drums rolled.

A whistle blew.

A parade began . . .

This parade felt different.
Not like the Fourth of July or Labor Day.

Many of the people on the big, bright floats
looked like me.

Marching bands high-stepped.
Played songs I recognized from the radio.

Soulful rhythms echoed differently.

Beauty queens' hands outstretched.

Decorated cars and trucks honked.

Candy was tossed right and left.

Boys and girls my size,
   some bigger,
      some with different colored eyes,
         scrambled to get treats.

Some moonwalked and danced.
Cameras caught the action.

I caught red, white, and blue beads.
Long plastic necklaces.

JUNETEENTH!

Everyone was happy.
Rejoicing in the ending of slavery in Texas.

A national holiday.

A *Freedom Day* that would last until night,
from *The Strand* to the seawall,
as the light bounced off the faces of so many.

I searched the crowd and focused.
Saw a man who looked like Paw-Paw.
A white beard and shiny eyes.
There was a lady who looked like Mimi.
A gentle smile and smooth hands
holding a snow cone.

There are so many people who look like us, I said,
as the smell of barbecued chicken and sausage flavored the air.

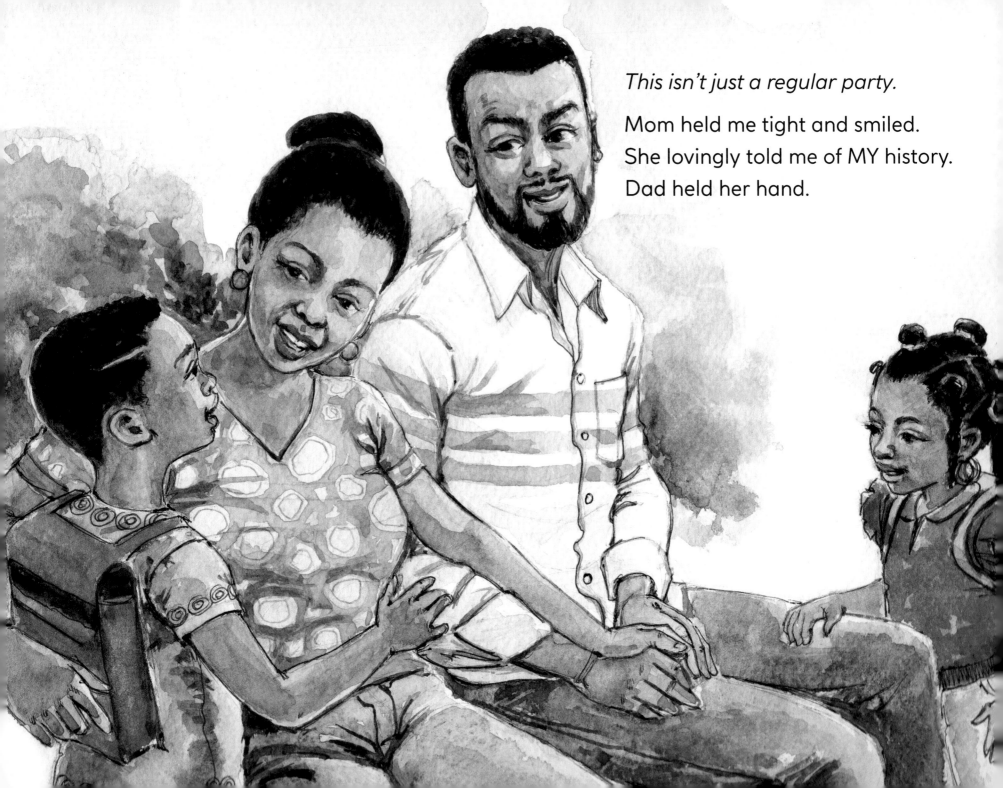

This isn't just a regular party.

Mom held me tight and smiled.
She lovingly told me of MY history.
Dad held her hand.

She told me about what my ancestors had experienced:

abuse and pain—heartache.
Facing the rising sun . . .
And how they overcame.
. . . till victory is won.

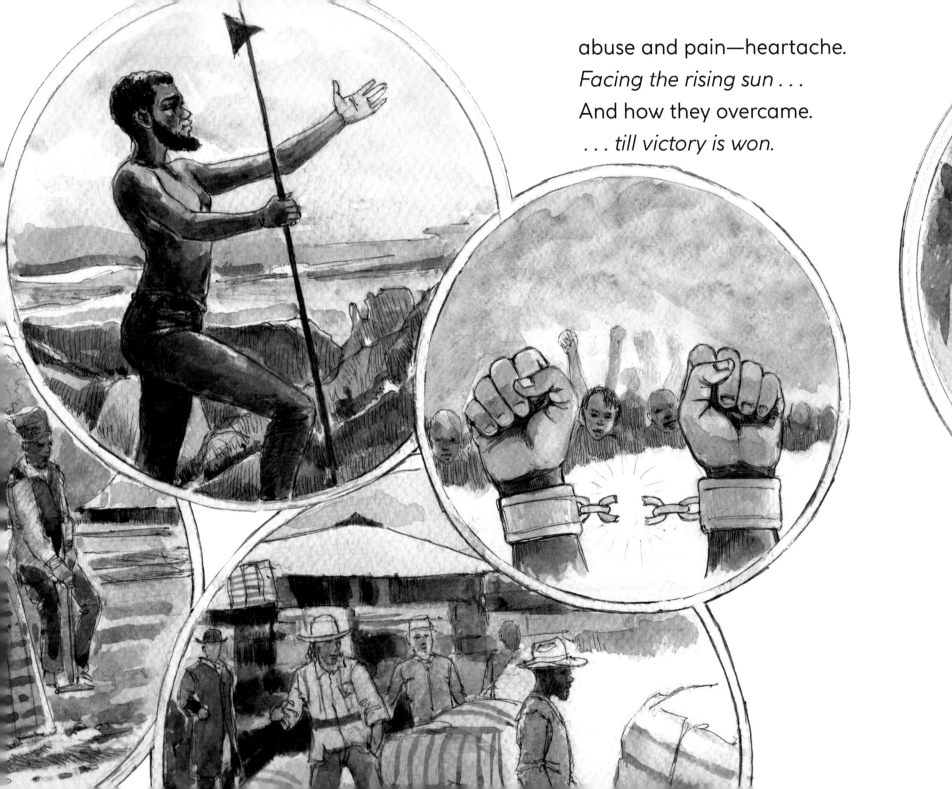

I understood why it's important to celebrate.

Sing a song
full of the
hope that the
present has
brought us.

Why we drove the miles
and strangers smiled.
Proud to have escaped
the nightmares.

Out from the gloomy past . . .

Why fireworks fell slowly over the ocean
as a crowd became a mass choir
that sang the *Negro National Anthem.*

Loud as the rolling sea . . .

Author's Note

When I was a kid, my parents took my sister and me to a Juneteenth parade in Grimes County.

Standing beside the tailgate of our truck, we watched Black cowboys and cowgirls tip their hats as they rode tall, beautiful horses and waved at the crowd. We heard the booming sounds of marching bands. Freshly washed cars and trucks gleamed and cruised in formation in the bright summer sun. Our noses loved the smells of cotton candy, funnel cakes, and turkey legs as we drank Big Red sodas, careful not to spill any on our *nice* clothes.

However, what I remember most was the pride that everyone had: Pride in the past. The present. And the future.

Strangers spoke to strangers. Families and friends shook hands, tightly hugged, and fellowshipped, like at church, but completely different at the same time, laughing in ways that filled the air with joy like songs and colorful balloons.

It was the type of day that I wanted to last forever—*Juneteenth*. Surrounded by people who knew me, as well as those who did not, but who loved me and my history all the same.

I hope that readers, especially young readers, feel proud, excited, and happy when they read this book! I hope that my words create joy about the most significant holiday that celebrates freedom and hope!

The ending of slavery!
JUNETEENTH!

—Van G. Garrett

Artists' Note

I was the little boy who loved to draw, who never grew up. Thanks to a very supportive family and broad network of friends and supporters, I've been fortunate to live the dream of becoming a professional artist. Pursuing this lifelong dream put me in a position to paint a big mural called *Absolute Equality* in Galveston, Texas, the birthplace of Juneteenth. The mural, which appears in this story, honors the rich history and heritage of Juneteenth.

Absolute Equality became the face of a national holiday and put me on the path to co-illustrate this book about Juneteenth as experienced through the eyes of a young boy and his family.

I hope this book inspires a new generation of children to embrace their own history and celebrate the power of freedom, liberation, and emancipation. My wish is that anyone who reads it or enjoys these illustrations understands that all dreams are possible and that the future belongs to those who never give up on their aspirations.

Cheers to Juneteenth and Absolute Equality for one and for ALL.

—Reginald C. Adams

When I was little, drawing and coloring was my escape. As a professional artist, I have worked on many important projects, but I feel most connected to the *Absolute Equality* mural and this book, which give me the chance to inspire the next generation.

May this book kindle in readers young or old the power to dream and the resilience to see the fulfillment of those dreams. Remember that your power is within, not without.

—Samson Bimbo Adenugba

For my Parents, Grandparents, and Great-Grandparents —V.G.G.

To my sons, Jahlani and Zenith Adams; my wife, Rhonda; my brother, Richard; my mother, Doris, and father, Charles; and all of my ancestors who I stand on the shoulders of. Thank you!
—R.C.A.

To my children, Precious, David, Joseph, Daniel, and Damilola; my sister, Nike; my lovely mum, Mrs. Ayoka Adenugba; and my late father, Samuel Olabode Adenugba. I appreciate your support. Finally, to the God of mercy, favor, and grace, thank you. —S.B.A.

Versify® is an imprint of HarperCollins Publishers.

Juneteenth
Text copyright © 2023 by Van G. Garrett
Illustrations copyright © 2023 by Reginald C. Adams and Samson Bimbo Adenugba
All rights reserved. Printed in the United States of America. No part of this book may be used or reproduced in any manner whatsoever without written permission except in the case of brief quotations embodied in critical articles and reviews. For information address HarperCollins Children's Books, a division of HarperCollins Publishers, 195 Broadway, New York, NY 10007.
www.harpercollinschildrens.com

Library of Congress Cataloging-in-Publication Data
Names: Garrett, Van G., author. | Adams, Reginald C., illustrator.
| Adenugba, Samson Bimbo, illustrator.
Title: Juneteenth / written by Van G. Garrett ; illustrated by
Reginald C. Adams and Samson Bimbo Adenugba.
Description: First edition. | New York, NY : Versify, [2023] | Audience: Ages 4–8. | Audience: Grades K–1. | Summary: An African American family attends a modern-day Juneteenth parade in Galveston, Texas (the birthplace of the holiday). Text includes lines from "Lift Every Voice and Sing."
Identifiers: LCCN 2022036208 | ISBN 9780358574323 (hardcover)
Subjects: LCSH: Juneteenth—Fiction. | CYAC: African Americans—Fiction. | Galveston (Tex.)—Fiction. | Parades—Fiction. | Family life—Fiction. | LCGFT: Picture books.
Classification: LCC PZ7.1.G37634 Ju 2023 | DDC [E]—dc23
LC record available at https://lccn.loc.gov/2022036208

The artists used water color and pen and ink on 140 pound archival water color paper to create the illustrations in this book.
Design by Whitney Leader-Picone
23 24 25 26 27 PHX 10 9 8 7 6 5 4 3 2 1

First Edition